AF228571

CHEVROLET CAMARO

Jessica Rusick

Big Buddy Books

An Imprint of Abdo Publishing
abdobooks.com

abdobooks.com

Published by Abdo Publishing, a division of ABDO, PO Box 398166, Minneapolis, Minnesota 55439. Copyright © 2021 by Abdo Consulting Group, Inc. International copyrights reserved in all countries. No part of this book may be reproduced in any form without written permission from the publisher. Big Buddy Books™ is a trademark and logo of Abdo Publishing.

Printed in the United States of America, North Mankato, Minnesota
082020
012021

THIS BOOK CONTAINS RECYCLED MATERIALS

Design: Christa Schneider, Mighty Media, Inc.
Production: Mighty Media, Inc.
Editor: Megan Borgert-Spaniol

Cover Photograph: Shutterstock Images

Interior Photographs: Amit Belani/Wikimedia Commons, pp. 16, 17; Arturo Pardavila III/ Wikimedia Commons, pp. 18, 19; dave_7/Flickr, pp. 14, 15; Library of Congress/Flickr, pp. 8, 9; Shutterstock Images, pp. 4, 5, 7, 10, 11, 12, 13, 20, 21, 22, 23, 26, 27, 28, 29; Sicnag/Flickr, pp. 28 (1966), 29 (2010); sv1ambo/Flickr, pp. 24, 25; Tacoma Public Library/Wikimedia Commons, p. 9 (Louis Chevrolet)

Design Elements: Shutterstock Images

Library of Congress Control Number: 2020931632

Publisher's Cataloging-in-Publication Data
Names: Rusick, Jessica, author.
Title: Chevrolet Camaro / by Jessica Rusick
Description: Minneapolis, Minnesota : Abdo Publishing, 2021 | Series: Mighty muscle cars | Includes online resources and index
Identifiers: ISBN 9781532193231 (lib. bdg.) | ISBN 9781098211875 (ebook)
Subjects: LCSH: Muscle cars--Juvenile literature. | Motor vehicles--Juvenile literature. | Automobiles--Customizing--Juvenile literature. | Hot rods--Juvenile literature.
Classification: DDC 629.222--dc23

CONTENTS

CAMARO V. MUSTANG

It's a clear, sunny day in Tucson, Arizona. A Chevrolet Camaro and a Ford Mustang rev their engines at the starting line. Then, tires screech. The race has begun!

Both cars zip down the track. The Camaro's engine roars. The cars race side by side for one-quarter mile (0.4 km). At the last second, the Camaro pulls ahead. The crowd cheers. The Camaro has won!

DID YOU KNOW?

In a drag race, two cars race on a straight track called a drag strip. Most drag strips are one-eighth mile (0.2 km) or one-quarter mile (0.4 km) long.

AMERICAN MUSCLE

The Chevrolet Camaro is among the most popular muscle cars. Muscle cars are American high-performance cars. They are built for power and speed.

The first muscle car came out in 1949. Muscle cars soon became widely popular in the 1960s. They were made for drag racing. But most could also be driven on city streets.

DID YOU KNOW?

Horsepower (hp) is a measure of how powerful an engine is. One hp equals the power needed to lift a 550-pound (249 kg) weight up one foot (0.3 m) in one second.

CHEVROLET CAMARO
FAST FACTS

Manufacturer: Chevrolet, a division of General Motors (GM)

First model year: 1967

Top speed: 198 mph (319 km/h)

Top horsepower: 650 hp

Top acceleration: 0 to 60 miles per hour (96 km/h) in 3.5 seconds

MICHIGAN MADE

The Chevrolet Camaro was born in Detroit, Michigan. Chevrolet Motor Company was founded there in 1911 by race car driver Louis Chevrolet and William C. Durant. Durant also founded General Motors (GM). In 1918, Chevrolet became part of GM.

Chevrolet soon became known for making popular, affordable cars and trucks. In the 1960s, Chevrolet would build a new kind of car.

William C. Durant
Louis Chevrolet

PONY CAR SHOWDOWN

In 1964, automaker Ford had just **debuted** the Mustang. This model marked a whole new class of cars called pony cars. These are small, fast, and sporty.

Chevrolet wanted to build its own pony car. The company wanted this new car to drive faster, run smoother, and handle better than the Mustang.

DID YOU KNOW?

Chevrolet called its pony car project "Project Panther." The Camaro was almost called the Panther!

More than 600,000 Ford Mustangs were sold in the car's first year.

THE FIRST GENERATION

In 1966, Chevrolet **debuted** the Camaro. Buyers chose between three different Camaro packages. These were the RS, the SS, and the Z28. Each had different special features.

The Z28 and the SS were built for racing. They had powerful engines and **transmissions**. In 1967 and 1969, the Camaro SS was the **pace car** at the Indianapolis 500 race.

A 1967 Chevrolet Camaro

NEXT GENS

The second-**generation** Camaro **debuted** in 1970. It sported a new body **design** and the comforts of a **luxury car**. The 1979 Camaro was especially popular. Chevrolet sold 282,571 of these cars!

From 1982 to 1993, Chevrolet came out with two more generations of Camaros. But buyers' tastes were changing. From 1990 to 2000, sports car sales fell. The Camaro was no longer selling. Chevrolet stopped making it in 2002.

During its second generation, the Camaro outsold the Ford Mustang for the first time.

CAMARO COMEBACK

The Camaro soon made a comeback. In 2006, Chevrolet **debuted** a Camaro **concept car** at an auto show in Detroit. People loved the new car. In 2010, a similar model became Chevrolet's fifth-**generation** Camaro.

In 2012, Chevrolet debuted the Camaro ZL1. This model was the fastest and most powerful Camaro yet. It would become a favorite on the racetrack!

The 2006 Camaro concept car was designed by South Korean designer SangYup Lee.

SIXTH GENERATION

In 2015, Chevrolet **debuted** its sixth-**generation** Camaro. The car was hundreds of pounds lighter than earlier models! It was also smaller. These changes helped the car handle better and drive faster.

For the Camaro's 50th **anniversary**, Chevrolet also made a special-**edition** Camaro. The metallic gray car featured cool **decals** on the hood and trunk.

A special-edition Camaro for the car's 50th anniversary

UNDER THE HOOD

CHEVROLET CAMARO ZL1

There are several types of the Camaro ZL1. The most powerful has a **supercharged** V8 engine. The *V8* means it has eight **cylinders**. Other Camaro models have V6 engines. The more cylinders an engine has, the more powerful it is.

CAR ENGINES 101

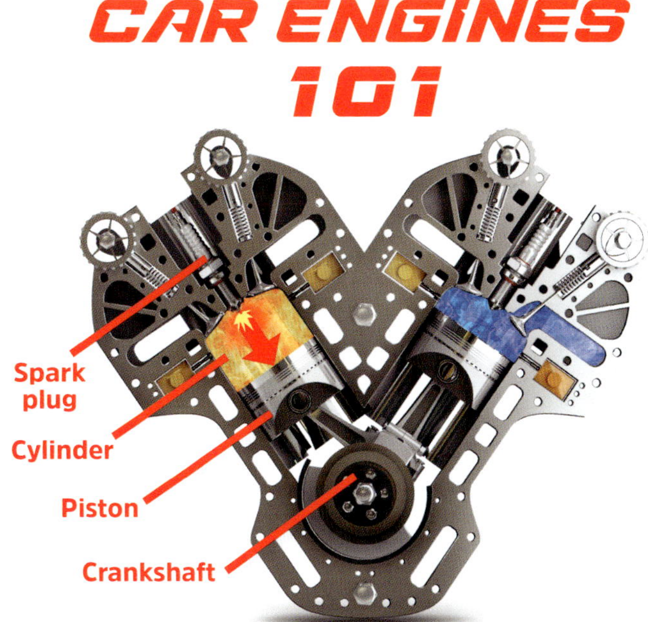

Car engines turn the energy in gasoline into motion. Fuel and air are pumped into the engine's **cylinders**. A spark creates an explosion. The explosion pushes the **piston** down to turn the **crankshaft**. This is a bit like a foot pushing down on a bicycle pedal. At high speed, these explosions happen thousands of times a minute!

TAKING TITLES

Camaros are popular on the racetrack. They are especially popular in drag racing! In 2017 and 2019, drag racer Robert Hight won several titles with his Camaro SS.

Camaros have also won titles in **NASCAR**. The Camaro ZL1 made its NASCAR **debut** in 2018. That same year, Austin Dillon won the Daytona 500 in a ZL1 Camaro!

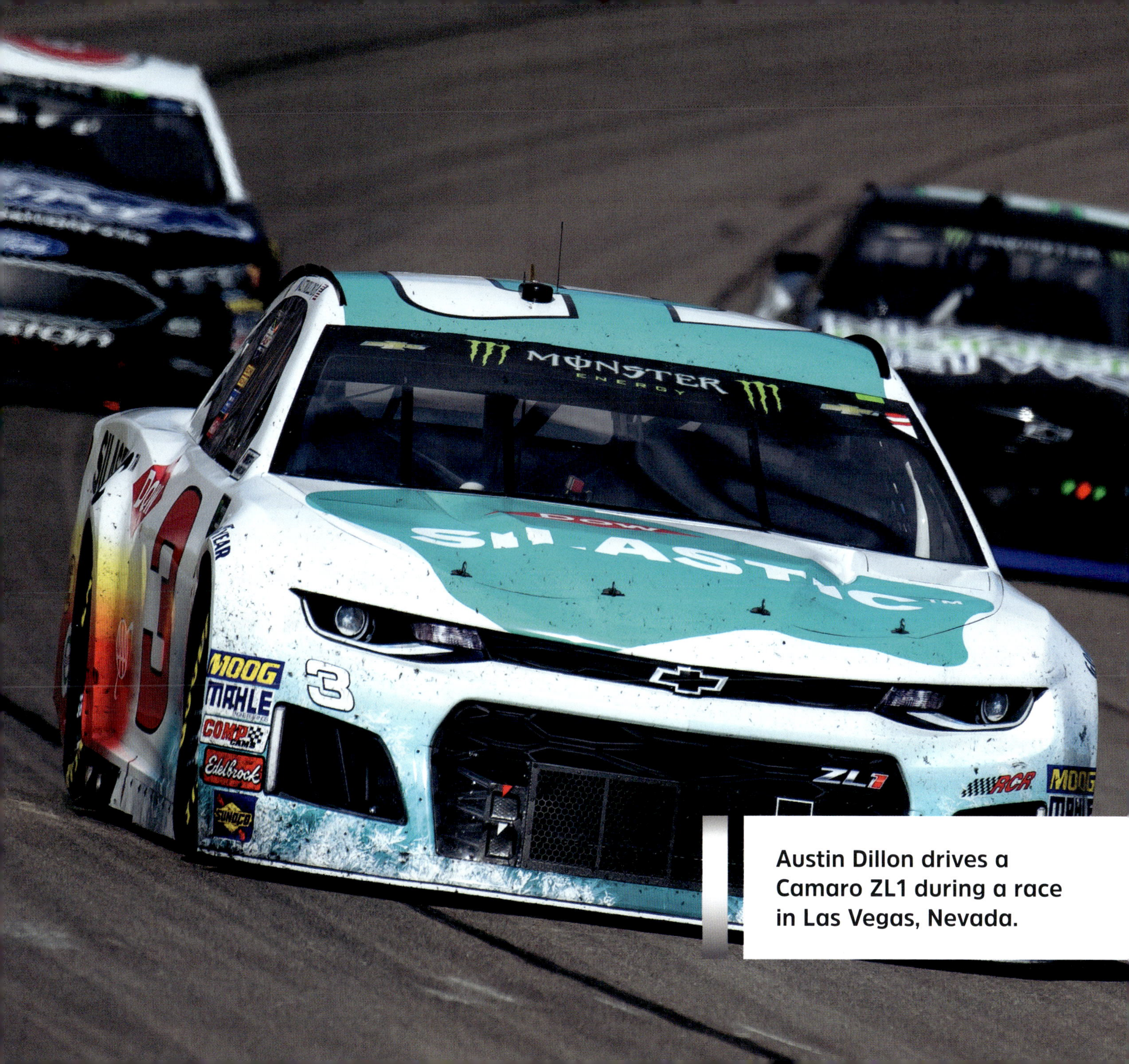

Austin Dillon drives a Camaro ZL1 during a race in Las Vegas, Nevada.

BIG-SCREEN BUMBLEBEE

Camaros have been featured in many movies. In 2013, a 1967 Camaro appeared in *Fast & Furious 6*. In 2015, a 1967 Camaro also appeared in the movie *Furious 7*.

The Camaro is most famous for its role in the *Transformers* films. The character Bumblebee takes the form of several different Camaros.

DID YOU KNOW?

The popularity of the *Transformers* movies helped Camaros become popular with young drivers.

In 2010, Chevrolet released a special *Transformers* Camaro. It was painted yellow and black, like the character Bumblebee.

RIDING ON

The Camaro continues to ride strong and fast. The 2019 Camaro had more special features than ever before. These included a touchscreen, heated steering wheel, and much more.

For some, the Camaro's future is uncertain. Car **experts** think Chevrolet may stop making the Camaro by 2023. No matter what the future holds, the Chevrolet Camaro will always be a favorite muscle car.

The 2019 Camaro SS has a V8 engine and up to 455 horsepower.

TIMELINE

Louis Chevrolet and William C. Durant founded Chevrolet Motor Company.

1911

Chevrolet **debuted** its first-**generation** Camaro.

1966

Chevrolet released its third-generation Camaro.

1982

1918

Chevrolet became part of General Motors (GM).

1970

Chevrolet introduced its second-generation Camaro.

Chevrolet **debuted** its fourth-generation Camaro.

1993

Chevrolet released its fifth-generation Camaro.

2010

2002

Chevrolet stopped making Camaros.

2015

Chevrolet debuted its sixth-generation Camaro.

GLOSSARY

anniversary—the date of a special event that is often celebrated each year.

concept car—a car produced as a model to show a new style or technology but not made available for sale.

crankshaft—a long, metal rod that transfers energy from the engine through the transmission and eventually to the wheels.

cylinder—a shaft in which a piston of an engine moves.

debut—to appear for the first time or present something for the first time. A debut is a first appearance.

decal—a label or sticker with a picture or design on it.

design (dih-ZINE)—a plan for how something will appear or work.

edition—a version of a product.

expert—a person very knowledgeable about a certain subject.

generation—a class of objects created from an earlier type.

luxury car—a car that provides drivers and other riders with a high level of comfort and quality.

NASCAR—the National Association for Stock Car Auto Racing.

pace car—a car that leads competing race cars during warm-up laps. A pace car also enters the track during a race to slow the pace if there are hazardous conditions.

piston—a part in an engine that moves up and down inside the cylinder.

supercharged—powered by a supercharger. A supercharger is a device that pushes more air into the engine to create a bigger explosion.

transmission—the part of a car that sends energy from the engine to the wheels.

ONLINE RESOURCES

To learn more about the Chevrolet Camaro, please visit **abdobooklinks.com** or scan this QR code. These links are routinely monitored and updated to provide the most current information available.

INDEX